The Berenstain Bears

WHEN I GROW UP

Now come with us
and you shall see
the many things
that you can be!

Mike Berenstain

Based on the characters created by Stan and Jan Berenstain

HARPER FESTIVAL
An Imprint of HarperCollinsPublishers

Library of Congress Control Number: 2015932000 • ISBN 978-0-06-235005-3
17 18 19   SCP   10 9 8 7 6 • ❖ • First Edition

Papa Bear showed his woodworking skills.

Mama displayed her quilts and told about her quilt shop.

Too-Tall Grizzly's dad, Two-Ton, explained how he ran a junkyard with his wife, Too-Too.

Grizzly Gramps and Gran performed their old tap dancing routine.

Finally, Ferdy Factual's uncle, Professor Actual Factual, told them about being a scientist. He showed them his telescope for studying the stars.

He showed them his microscope for studying tiny germs.

He did a chemistry experiment that made a bad smell. He showed them real fossils from a dinosaur dig. It was all very interesting.

As the cubs walked home after school, Sister was thoughtful.

"Brother," she said, "do you know what you want to be when you grow up?"

"Sure!" he said, bouncing a soccer ball off his head. "A soccer star."

But Sister wasn't so sure. She had many interests—books, music, nature, science, art, and sports. She could be almost anything. As they walked, Professor Actual Factual and Nephew Ferdy drove by in the Actual-Factualmobile.

"Hello, Professor! Hello, Ferdy!" said Brother and Sister.

"Would you like a lift?" asked the professor. "You can use my cell phone to ask your mama and papa."

"Thank you!" they said, and called Mama and Papa before climbing aboard.

"How did you like Career Day?" asked the professor. "Did it give you any ideas about what you'd like to be when you grow up?"

"Yes," said Sister, "*too* many! There are so many jobs to choose from."

"Good point," said the professor. "Maybe we should take a tour of Bear Country to learn about different kinds of jobs."

"That would be great!" said Sister.

"Sounds like fun," said Brother.

"One Actual Factual Job Tour coming up!" said the professor, first picking up his phone to okay the trip with Mama and Papa. "Now look around," he said. "What sorts of jobs do we see? Carpenter, painter, mail carrier, cook—everyone is hard at work."

"Uh-oh!" said the professor, rounding a bend. "What's all this?"

"Wow!" said the cubs. "A fire!"

Fire trucks, police cars, and ambulances blocked the way. Smoke was coming from a building.

"Say!" said the professor. "You might be a firefighter. You could ride on a big, red truck and save lives. You might even save someone's pet! I'm sure no one will mind if they get a bit damp. Or you could be a policebear or an emergency worker and keep everyone safe."

They drove past the Bear Country Airport.

"I know you're really into airplanes, Brother—you, too, Sister," said the professor. "If your dream is flying, you could be airline pilots and fly a jumbo jet. Or you could fly even higher and really *go* someplace—outer space, to be exact. You could be an astronaut and blast off in a rocket to the stars."

The professor and the cubs passed a construction site where giant dump trucks and earth movers were digging and plowing, pushing and piling.

"On the other hand," said the professor, "you may decide to keep your feet on the ground. Try on a hard hat and put some megamachines through their paces. Now there's a job you could *dig*!" he added with a chuckle.

They drove into the countryside past Farmer Ben's farm.

"Farming is a very important job," he said. "Farmers grow the food we eat. Without them, we might starve!"

"Wow!" said the cubs. They had never thought about Farmer Ben like that before.

"Farmers grow all our wheat and corn, our vegetables and fruit. They raise farm animals like sheep, goats, pigs, chickens, ducks, and turkeys. Farmers work all day plowing, planting, weeding and harvesting, *and* . . . ," he added, "they still have time to milk the cows."

"Let's move a little faster," said the professor. "We have many more jobs to learn about."

He pulled a lever and a big propeller popped out of the Actual-Factualmobile. They took off and flew across Bear Country.

They flew over Big Bear High School. They saw teachers in their classrooms and coaches with their teams. They flew over Grizzly Medical Center. They saw doctors, nurses, dentists, and other health workers. They flew over downtown Grizzlytown. They saw shopkeepers, delivery bears, plumbers, sign painters, bus drivers, mechanics, road crews, and repairbears all busily at work.

"Perhaps," said the professor as they flew on, "you are more the artistic type. Maybe an artist's life is the life for you. You could paint pictures or become an author. You could act on the stage, dance in a ballet, play in an orchestra, or sing in an opera."

"There are many interesting and important jobs to be done," said the professor as he turned the Actual-Factualmobile toward home. "But there is one more very important job to learn about." They flew low over a neighborhood of family homes. "It's the job of parent—a mom or a dad. That may be about the most important job there is!"

The professor landed in the backyard of the Bear family's tree house. The big propeller folded back into the Actual-Factualmobile. Brother and Sister climbed down and waved good-bye.

"Good-bye!" called the professor as he and Ferdy drove away. "I hope you enjoyed our Bear Country job tour. When you think about what you want to be when you grow up, just remember this little rhyme:

So many different jobs to be done—
Just choose the right one and work can be fun!"